SPECTRUM®

Numbers & Counting

PreK–K

Published by Spectrum®
an imprint of Carson-Dellosa Publishing
Greensboro, NC

Spectrum®
An imprint of Carson-Dellosa Publishing LLC
P.O. Box 35665
Greensboro, NC 27425 USA

Printed in the USA • All rights reserved.   ISBN 978-1-4838-3103-9

01-053167784

Table of Contents Numbers & Counting

Lesson 1.1 Counting 0, 1, and 2

Count the number of objects out loud. Then, color the correct number.

Lesson 1.2 Writing 0, 1, and 2

Count the number of objects out loud. Trace the number. Write the number. Begin at ●.

2   ●

0   ●

1   ●

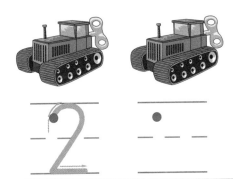

2   ●

2   ●

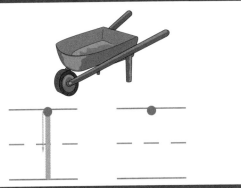

1   ●

0   ●

2   ●

Lesson 1.3 Counting 3 and 4

Circle the objects in each group to match the given number. Then, color the number.

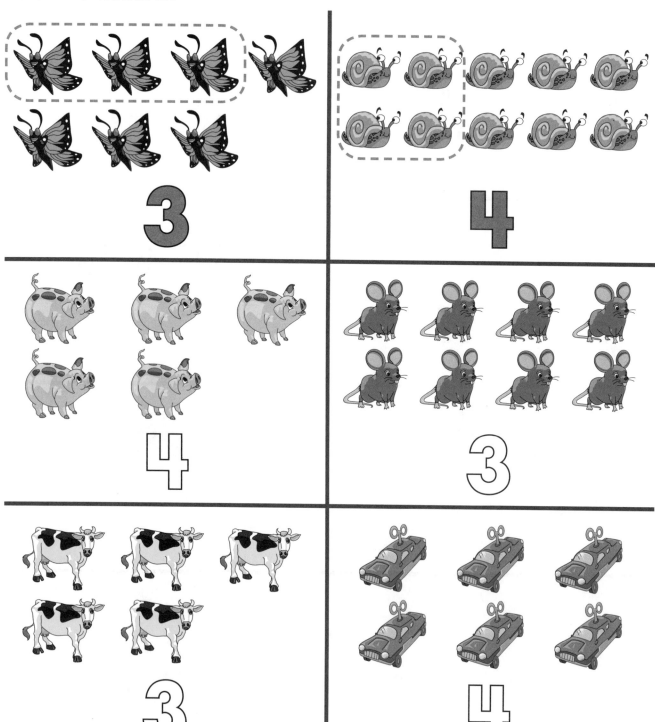

Lesson 1.4 Writing 3 and 4

Count the number of objects in each group out loud. Trace the number. Write the number. Begin at ●.

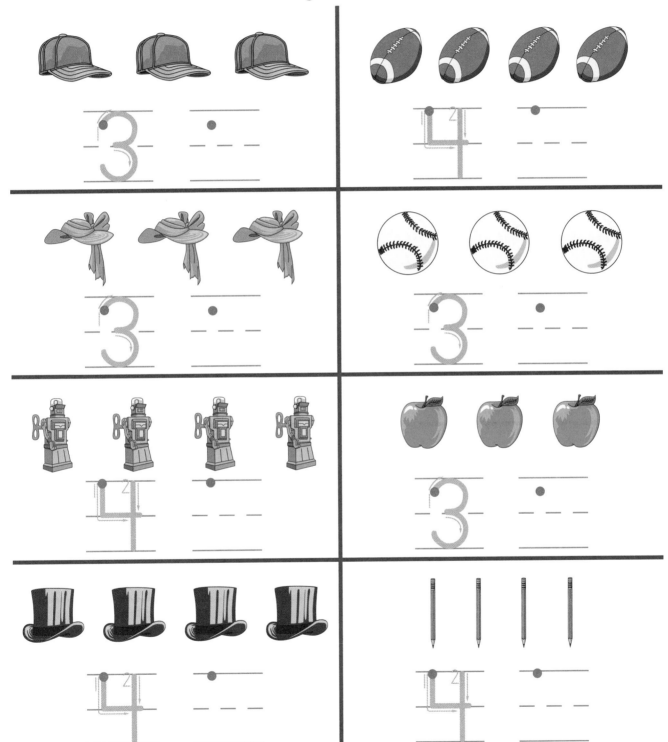

NAME _____

Lesson 1.5 Counting Through 4

Start from the number shown. Keep counting. Write the missing numbers.

0 ___ ___ ___

2 ___ ___ ___

1 ___ ___ ___

3 ___ ___

NAME _____

Lesson 1.6 Counting 5

Count the number of objects in each group out loud. Then, color the correct number.

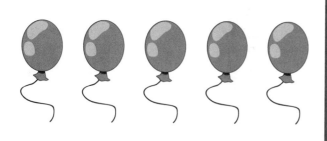

 3   **5**

 2   5

 4 5

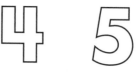 4 5

 3   5

 2 5

Lesson 1.7 Writing 5

Circle the objects to make 5. Trace the number. Write the number.
Begin at •.

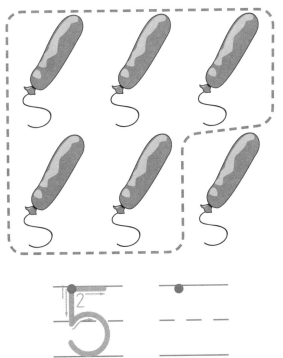

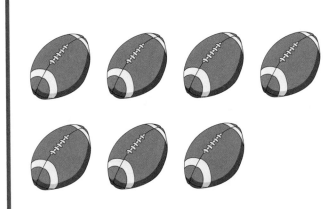

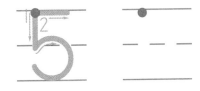

Lesson 1.8 Counting 6 and 7

Count the number of objects out loud. Then, color the correct number.

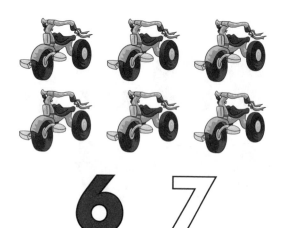

6 7

6 7

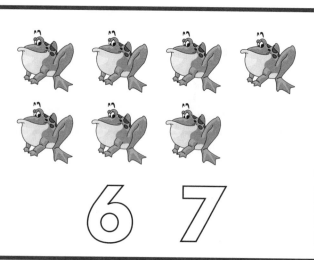

6 7

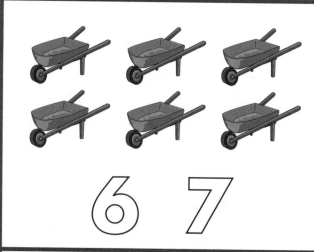

6 7

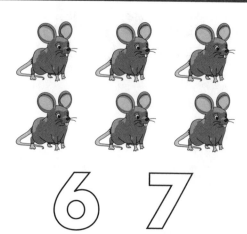

6 7

6 7

NAME _____

Lesson 1.9 Writing 6 and 7

Count the number of objects in each group out loud. Trace the number. Write the number. Begin at •.

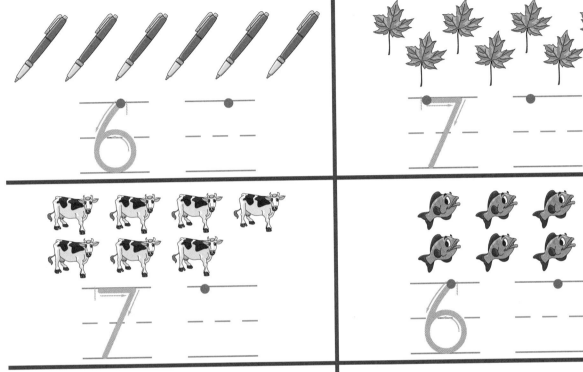

Lesson 1.10 Counting Through 7

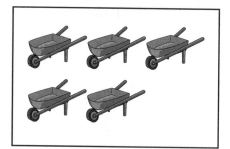 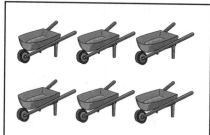 

five · · · · · · · · · · six · · · · · · · · · · seven

5 · · · · · · · · · · 6 · · · · · · · · · · 7

Circle the number.

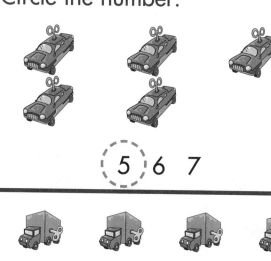

(5) 6 7

5 6 7

5 6 7

5 6 7

5 6 7

5 6 7

Lesson 1.10 Counting Through 7

Start from the number shown. Keep counting. Write the missing numbers.

3 ___ ___ ___

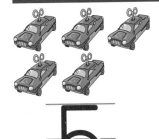  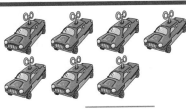 

5 ___ ___

4 ___ ___ ___

2 ___ ___ ___ ___

Lesson 1.11 Counting 8 and 9

Circle the objects to make the given number. Then, color the number.

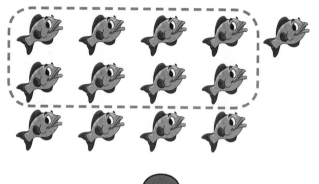

8

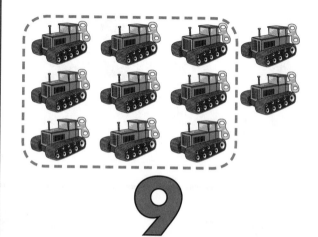

9

9

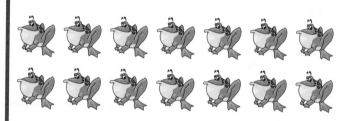

8

8

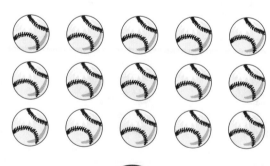

9

Lesson 1.12 Writing 8 and 9

Count the number of objects in each group out loud. Trace the number. Write the number. Begin at ●.

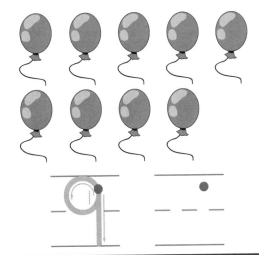

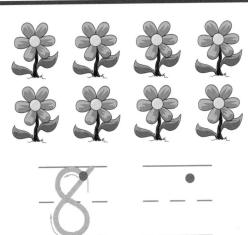

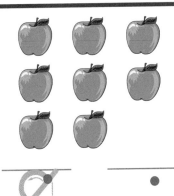

Lesson 1.13 Counting 10

Count the number of objects in each group out loud. Then, color the correct number.

 8   **10**

 9   10

 7   10

 8   10

 5   10

 6   10

Lesson 1.14 Writing 10

Cross out the extra objects in each group to make 10. Trace the number. Write the number. Begin at •.

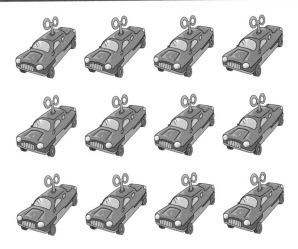

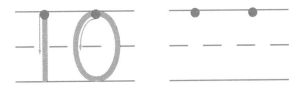

Lesson 1.15 Counting Through 10

eight	nine	ten
8	9	10

Circle the number.

8 (9) 10

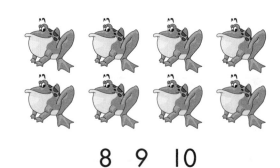

8 9 10

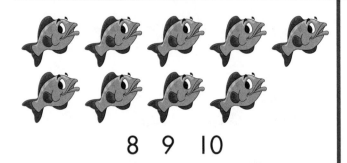

8 9 10

8 9 10

8 9 10

8 9 10

Lesson 1.15 Counting Through 10

Start from the number shown. Keep counting. Write the missing numbers.

5 ___ ___ ___ ___

8 ___ ___

7 ___ ___ ___

4 ___ ___ ___ ___

Lesson 1.16 Counting and Writing 0 Through 10

Count how many. Write the number.

_____ _ _ _ _____

_____ _ _ _ _____

_____ _ _ _ _____

_____ _ _ _ _____

_____ _ _ _ _____

_____ _ _ _ _____

_____ _ _ _ _____
_____ _ _ _ _____

_____ _ _ _ _____
_____ _ _ _ _____

NAME ________________________

Lesson 1.16 Counting and Writing 0 Through 10

Count how many. Write the number.

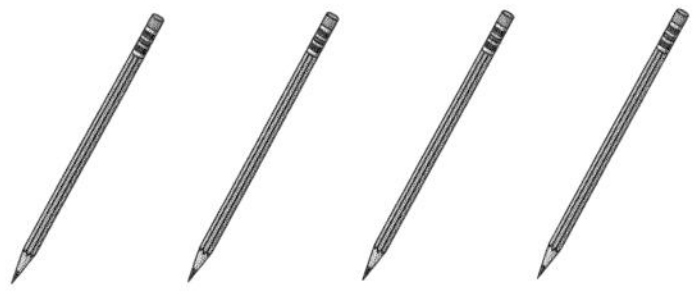

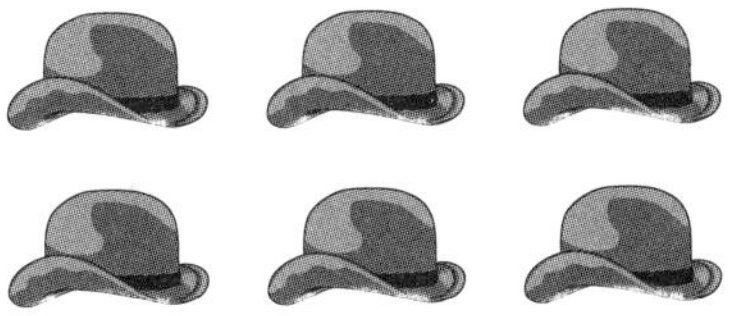

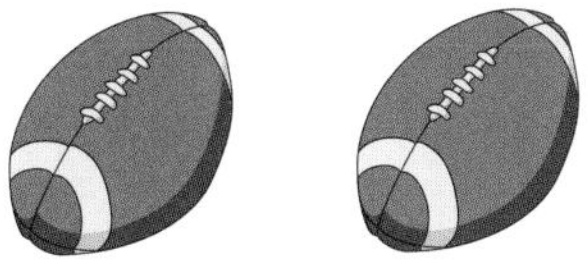

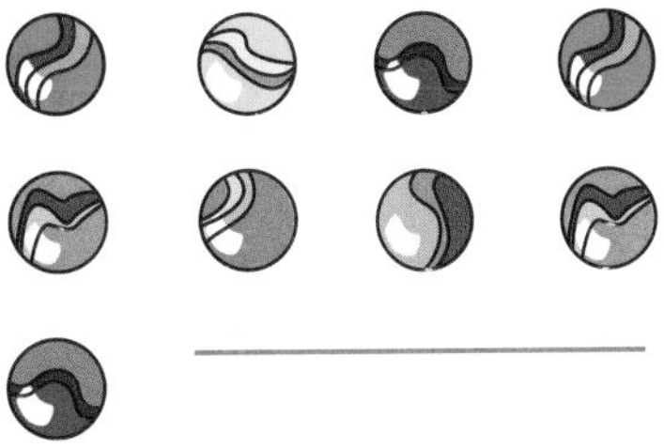

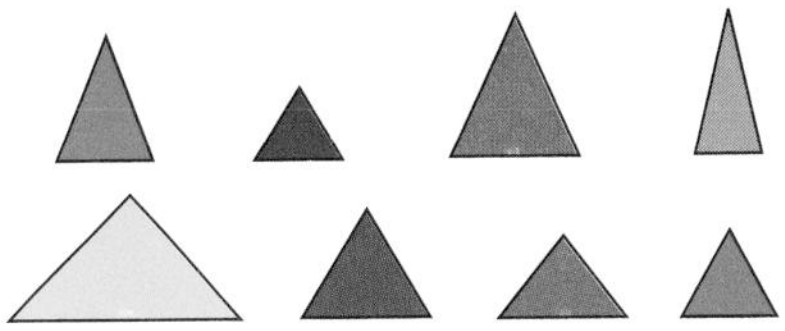

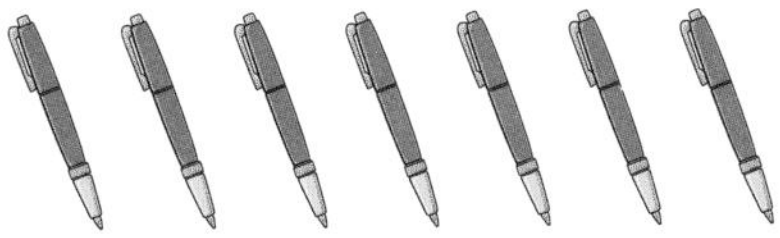

Lesson 1.16 Counting and Writing 0 Through 10

Count the 🧍. Say the number. Write the number.

_____ 6 _____

_____

_____

_____

_____

_____

_____

Lesson 1.16 Counting and Writing 0 Through 10

Count the 🤖. Say the number. Write the number.

Lesson 2.1 Counting and Writing 11

11 is 10 plus 1 more. Count 11 dots.

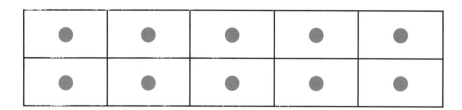

Draw a circle around 10 balloons. Count 11 balloons altogether.
Trace and write 11.

Lesson 2.2 Counting and Writing 12

12 is 10 plus 2 more. Count 12 dots.

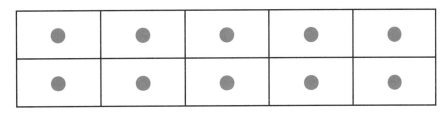

Draw a circle around 10 snails. Count 12 snails altogether. Trace and write 12.

Lesson 2.3 Counting Through 12

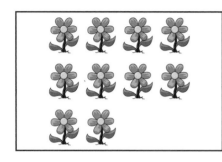
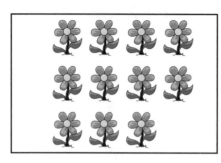
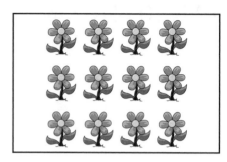

ten	eleven	twelve
10	11	12

Circle the number.

10 (11) 12

9   10   11

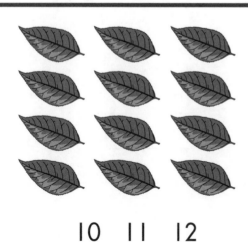

10   11   12

9   10   11

Lesson 2.3 Counting Through 12

Start from the number shown. Keep counting. Write the missing numbers.

8 ___ ___ ___ ___

5 ___ ___ ___ ___

10 ___ ___

7 ___ ___ ___ ___

9 ___ ___ ___

Lesson 2.4 Counting and Writing 13

13 is 10 plus 3 more. Count 13 dots.

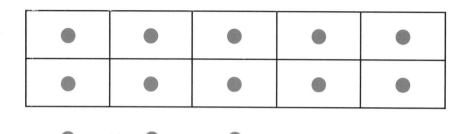

Draw a circle around 10 fish. Count 13 fish altogether. Trace and write 13.

Lesson 2.5 Counting and Writing 14

14 is 10 plus 4 more. Count 14 dots.

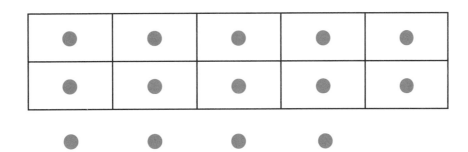

Draw a circle around 10 leaves. Count 14 leaves altogether.
Trace and write 14.

Lesson 2.6 Counting Through 14

twelve

12

thirteen

13

fourteen

14

Circle the number.

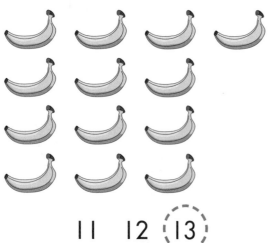

11   12   (13)

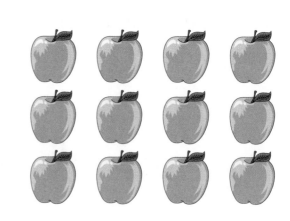

12   13   14

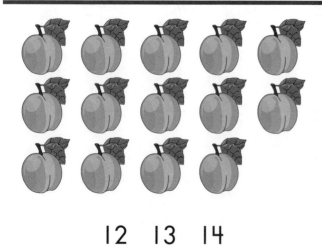

12   13   14

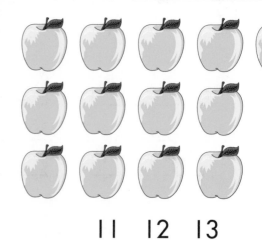

11   12   13

Lesson 2.6 Counting Through 14

Start from the number shown. Keep counting. Write the missing numbers.

10 ___ ___ ___ ___

9 ___ ___ ___ ___

3 ___ ___ ___ ___

5 ___ ___ ___ ___

11 ___ ___ ___

Lesson 2.7 Counting and Writing 15

15 is 10 plus 5 more. Count 15 dots.

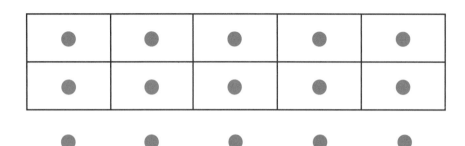

Draw a circle around 10 apples. Count 15 apples altogether.
Trace and write 15.

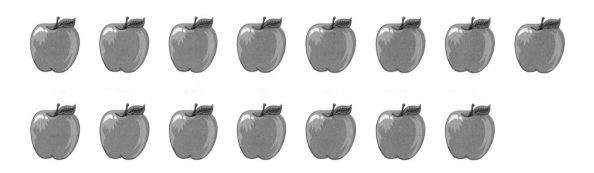

15 _ _ _ _ _ _

Lesson 2.8 Counting and Writing 16

16 is 10 plus 6 more. Count 16 dots.

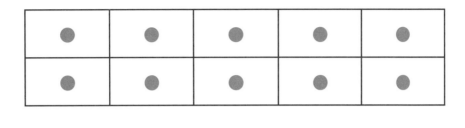

Draw a circle around 10 butterflies. Count 16 butterflies altogether. Trace and write 16.

16

Lesson 2.9 Counting Through 16

fourteen

14

fifteen

15

sixteen

16

Circle the number.

13 14 (15)

12 13 14

14 15 16

13 14 15

Lesson 2.9 Counting Through 16

Start from the number shown. Keep counting. Write the missing numbers.

12 ____ ____ ____ ____

10 ____ ____ ____ ____

11 ____ ____ ____ ____

9 ____ ____ ____ ____

0 ____ ____ ____ ____

Lesson 2.10 Counting and Writing 17

17 is 10 plus 7 more. Count 17 dots.

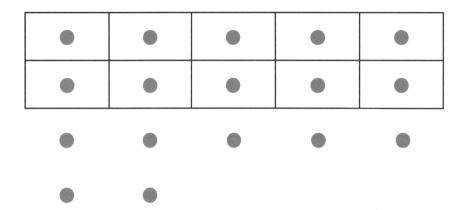

Draw a circle around 10 flowers. Count 17 flowers altogether.
Trace and write 17.

17 _ _ _ _ _ _ _

Lesson 2.11 Counting and Writing 18

18 is 10 plus 8 more. Count 18 dots.

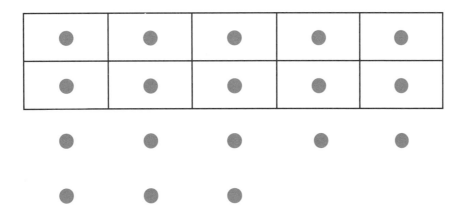

Draw a circle around 10 frogs. Count 18 frogs altogether. Trace and write 18.

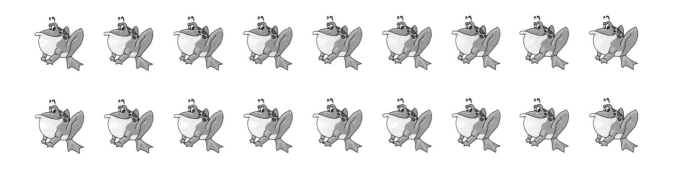

18

Lesson 2.12 Counting Through 18

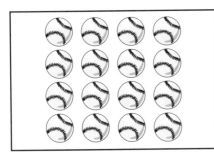 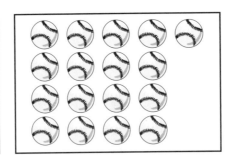 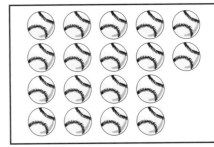

sixteen   seventeen   eighteen

16   17   18

Circle the number.

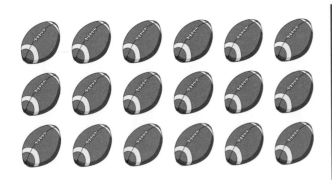

16   17   (18)

15   16   17

16   17   18

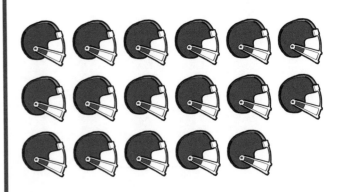

16   17   18

Lesson 2.12 Counting Through 18

Start from the number shown. Keep counting. Write the missing numbers.

10 ___ ___ ___ ___

14 ___ ___ ___ ___

3 ___ ___ ___ ___

13 ___ ___ ___ ___

9 ___ ___ ___ ___

Lesson 2.13 Counting and Writing 19

19 is 10 plus 9 more. Count 19 dots.

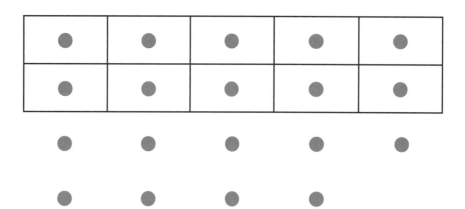

Draw a circle around 10 peaches. Count 19 peaches altogether.
Trace and write 19.

Lesson 2.14 Counting and Writing 20

20 is two groups of 10. Count 20 dots.

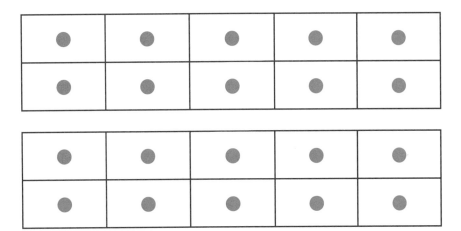

Draw a circle around each group of 10 canoes. Count 20 canoes altogether. Trace and write 20.

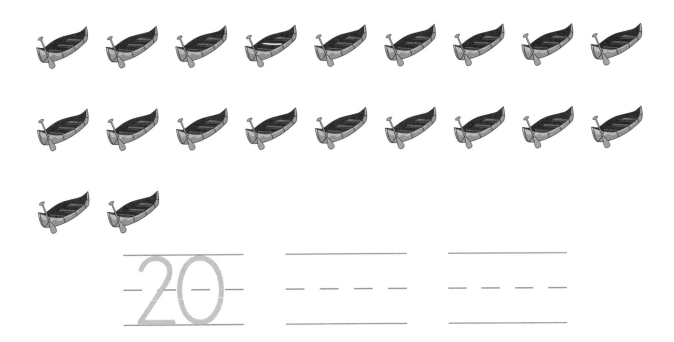

Lesson 2.15 Counting Through 20

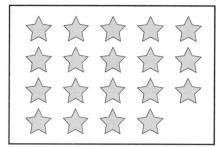

eighteen	nineteen	twenty
18	19	20

Circle the number.

18   19   (20)

15   16   17

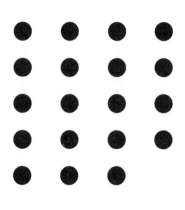

18   19   20

17   18   19

Lesson 2.15 Counting Through 20

Start from the number shown. Keep counting. Write the missing numbers.

13 ___ ___ ___ ___

16 ___ ___ ___ ___

12 ___ ___ ___ ___

8 ___ ___ ___ ___

2 ___ ___ ___ ___

Lesson 2.16 Counting and Writing 11 Through 20

Count how many. Trace the number.

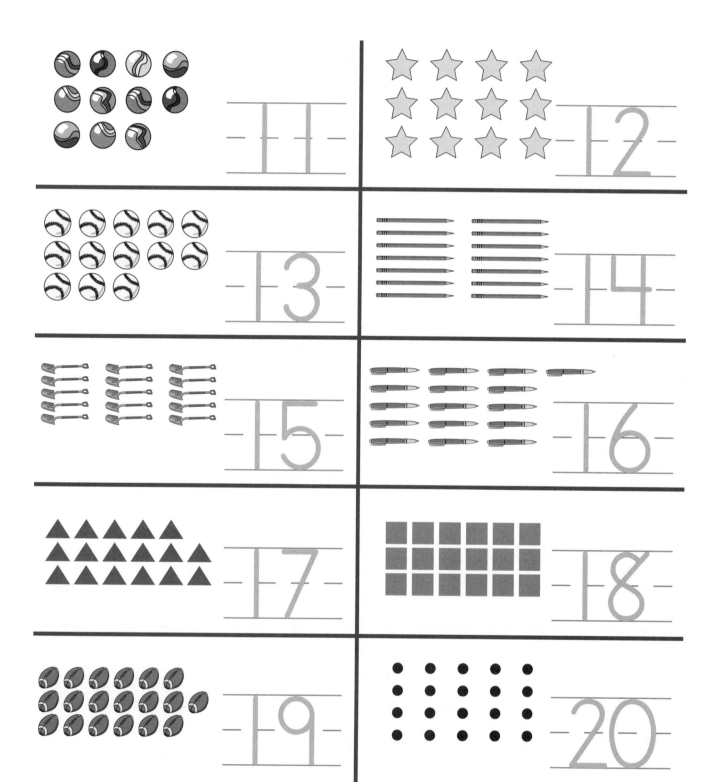

Lesson 2.16 Counting and Writing 11 Through 20

Count how many. Write the number.

_____

_____

_____

_____

_____

_____

_____

_____

_____

_____

Lesson 2.16 Counting and Writing 11 Through 20

Count the dots. Write the number.

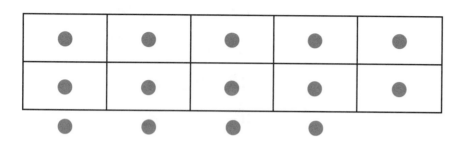 

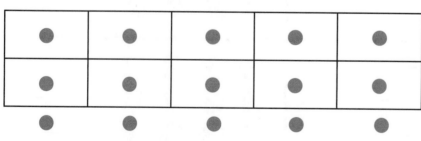

Lesson 2.16 Counting and Writing 11 Through 20

Count the dots. Write the number.

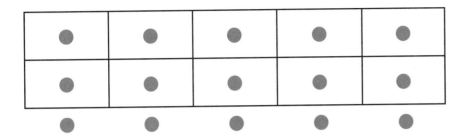

_____
- - - - - - -
_____

_____
- - - - - - -
_____

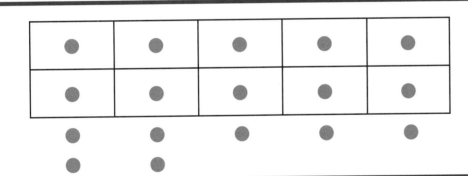

_____
- - - - - - -
_____

_____
- - - - - - -
_____

Lesson 3.1 Finding the Group That Is Greater

Greater means "more." Count the objects. In each pair, circle the group that is greater.

 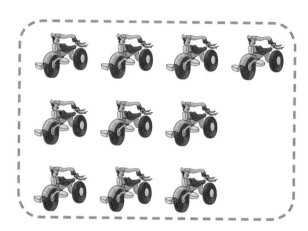

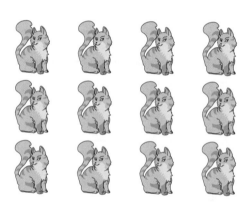 

Lesson 3.1 Finding the Group That Is Greater

Count the objects. In each pair, circle the group that is greater.

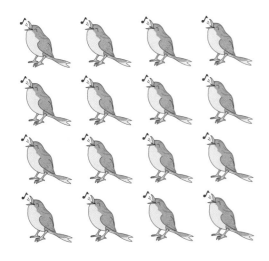 

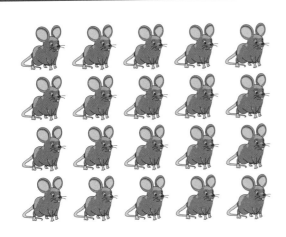 

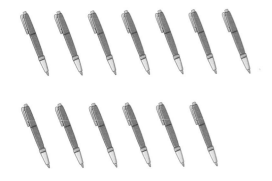 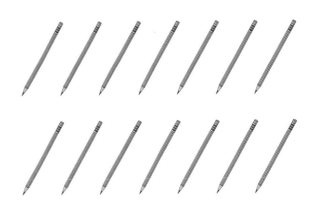

Lesson 3.2 Finding the Group With the Greater Number

Write a number to tell how many are in each group. Then, for each pair, circle the group that is greater.

7   10

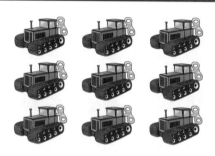   

_____   _____

   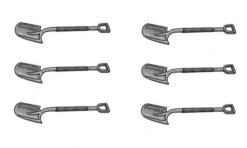

_____   _____

Lesson 3.2 Finding the Group With the Greater Number

Write a number to tell how many are in each group. Then, for each pair, circle the group that is greater.

_____

‒ ‒ ‒ ‒

_____

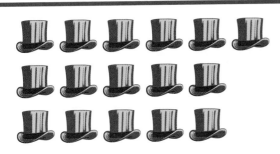   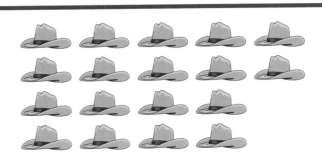

_____

‒ ‒ ‒ ‒

_____

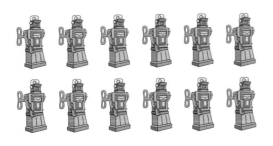   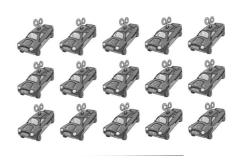

_____

‒ ‒ ‒ ‒

_____

Lesson 3.3 Classifying to Find Which Is Greater

How many? Write the number. Then, circle a picture to answer the question.

Which is greater?

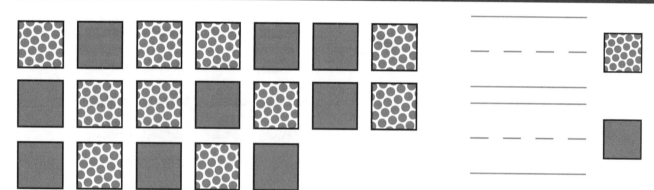

Which is greater?

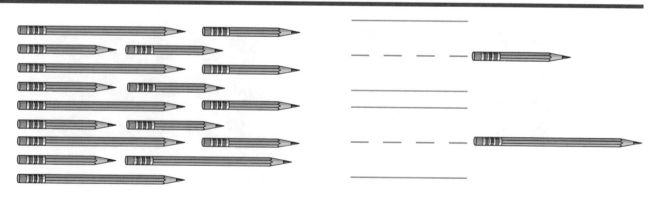

Which is greater?

Lesson 3.4 Finding the Number That Is Greater

In each pair, circle the number that is greater.

3	5	8	4
5	0	4	7
10	6	3	5
10	8	2	6

Lesson 3.5 Finding the Group That Is Less

Less means "fewer." Count the objects. In each pair, circle the group that is less.

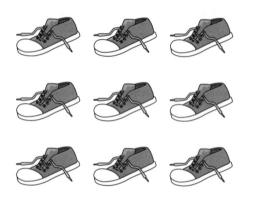

Lesson 3.5 Finding the Group That Is Less

Count the objects. In each pair, circle the group that is less.

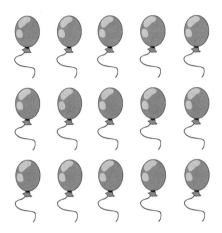 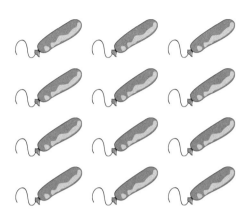

 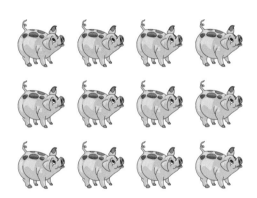

Lesson 3.6 Finding the Group With the Lesser Number

Write a number to tell how many are in each group. Then, for each pair, circle the group that is less.

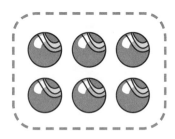

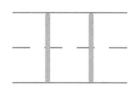

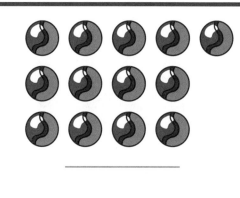

_____

_ _ _ _

_____

_ _ _ _

_____

_ _ _ _

_____

_____

_ _ _ _

_____

Lesson 3.6 Finding the Group With the Lesser Number

Write a number to tell how many are in each group. Then, for each pair, circle the group that is less.

_____

_ _ _ _ _

_____

_____

_ _ _ _ _

_____

_____

_ _ _ _ _

_____

_____

_ _ _ _ _

_____

_____

_ _ _ _ _

_____

_____

_ _ _ _ _

_____

Lesson 3.7 Classifying to Find Which Is Less

How many? Write the number. Then, circle a picture to answer the question.

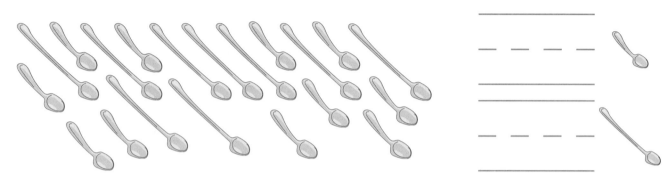

_____

Which is less?

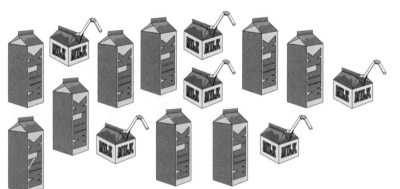

Which is less?

Which is less?

Lesson 3.8 Finding the Number That Is Less

In each pair, circle the number that is less.

6	7	10	5
5	8	3	0
7	9	0	4
8	5	1	10

Lesson 3.9 Finding Groups That Are Equal

Equal means "the same as." Count the objects. Draw lines to connect the groups that are equal.

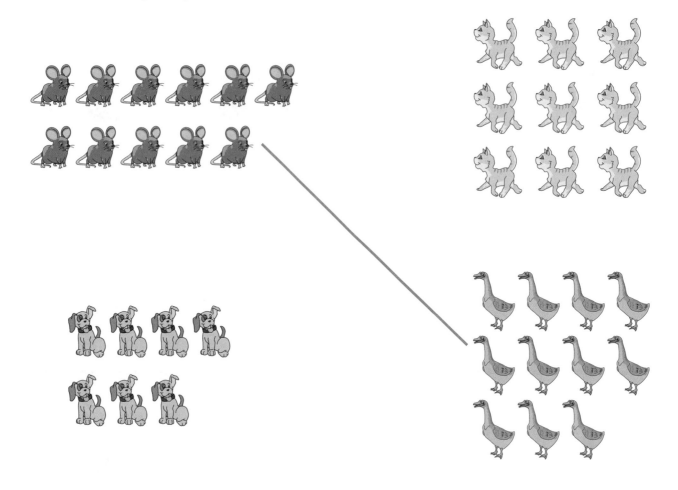

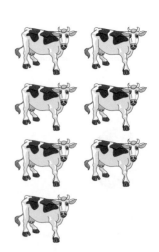

NAME _____

Lesson 3.9 Finding Groups That Are Equal

Count the objects. Draw lines to connect the groups that are equal.

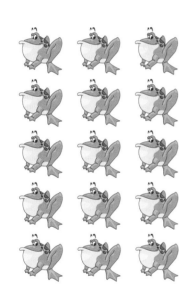

Lesson 3.10 Classifying to Find Groups That Are Equal

Count the animals. Write numbers and circle pictures to answer the questions.

How many ? _____

How many ? _____

How many ? _____

How many ? _____

How many ? _____

How many 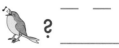? _____

Which groups are equal?

Which groups are equal?

NAME _____

Count the items of clothing. Write numbers and circle pictures to answer the questions.

_____

How many ? _____

How many ? _____

How many ? _____

How many ? _____

How many ? _____

How many ? _____

Which groups are equal?

Which groups are equal?

Lesson 4.1 Counting and Writing 30

30 is three groups of 10. Count 30 dots.

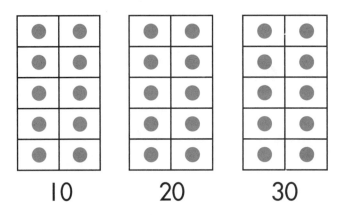

Count 30 apples. Circle each group of 10 apples. Draw a worm in apple 26.

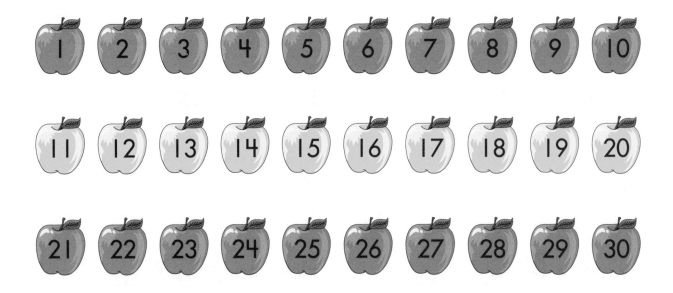

Trace and write 30.

Lesson 4.2 Counting and Writing 40

40 is four groups of 10. Count 40 dots.

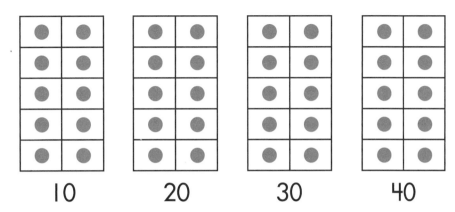

10   20   30   40

Count 40 apples. Circle each group of 10 apples. Draw a worm in apple 32.

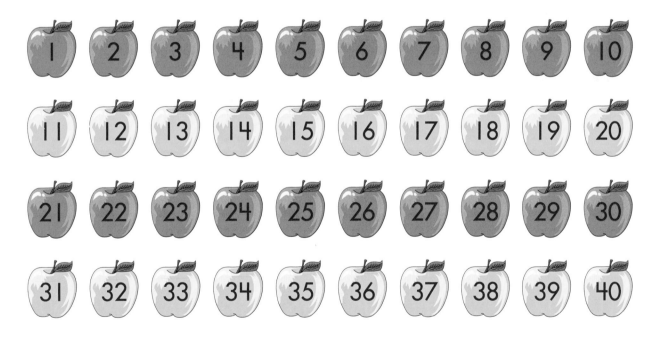

Trace and write 40.

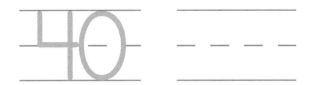

Lesson 4.3 Counting and Writing 50

50 is five groups of 10. Count 50 dots.

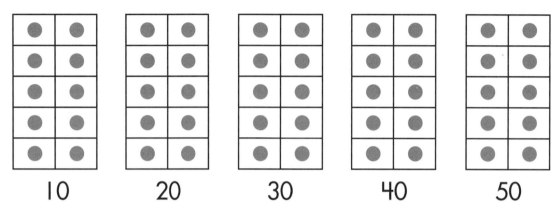

10   20   30   40   50

Count 50 apples. Circle each group of 10 apples. Draw a worm in apple 48.

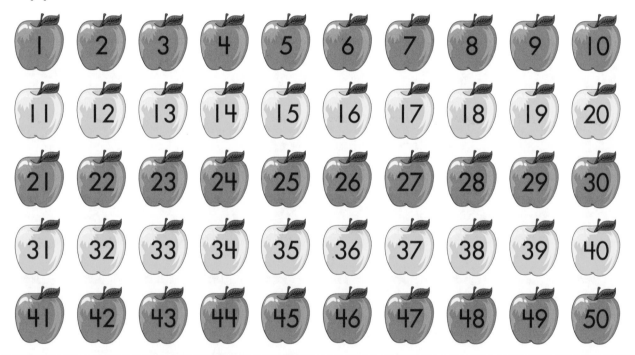

Trace and write 50.

Lesson 4.4 Counting and Writing 60

60 is six groups of 10. Count 60 dots.

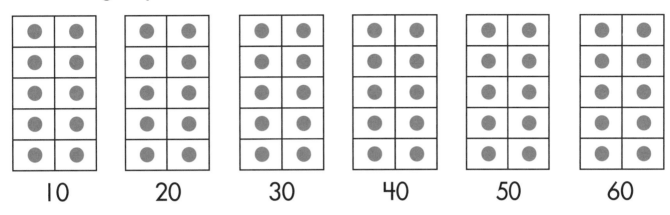

| 10 | 20 | 30 | 40 | 50 | 60 |

Count 60 apples. Circle each group of 10 apples. Draw a worm in apple 51.

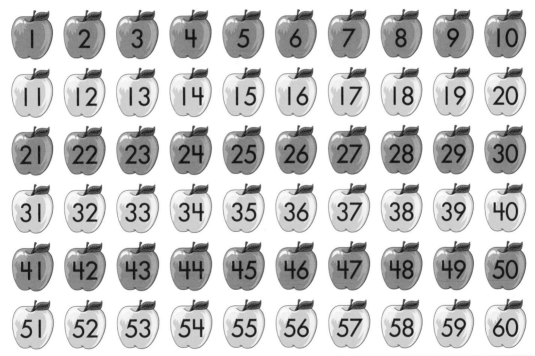

Trace and write 60.

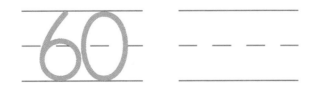

Lesson 4.5 Counting and Writing 70

70 is seven groups of 10. Count 70 dots.

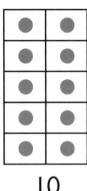 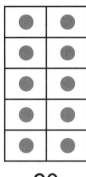 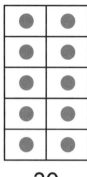 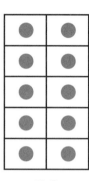

   10   20   30   40

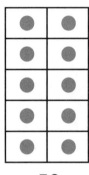 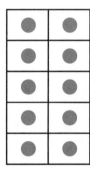 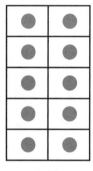

   50   60   70

Trace and write 70.

70 _ _ _

Lesson 4.5 Counting and Writing 70

Count 70 apples. Circle each group of 10 apples. Draw a worm in apple 63.

Lesson 4.6 Counting and Writing 80

80 is eight groups of 10. Count 80 dots.

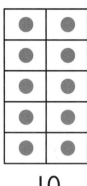
10

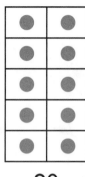
20

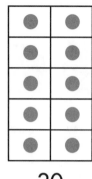
30

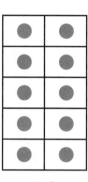
40

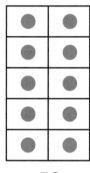
50

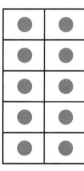
60

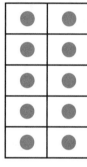
70

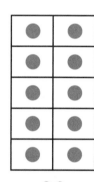
80

Trace and write 80.

Lesson 4.6 Counting and Writing 80

Count 80 apples. Circle each group of 10 apples. Draw a worm in apple 74.

1 2 3 4 5 6 7 8 9 10

11 12 13 14 15 16 17 18 19 20

21 22 23 24 25 26 27 28 29 30

31 32 33 34 35 36 37 38 39 40

41 42 43 44 45 46 47 48 49 50

51 52 53 54 55 56 57 58 59 60

61 62 63 64 65 66 67 68 69 70

71 72 73 74 75 76 77 78 79 80

Lesson 4.7 Counting and Writing 90

90 is nine groups of 10. Count 90 dots.

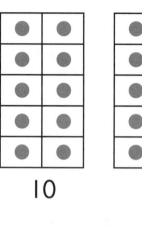 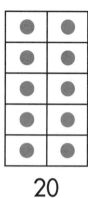 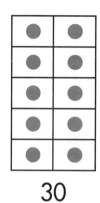 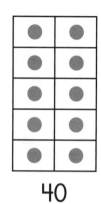 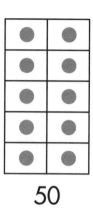

10   20   30   40   50

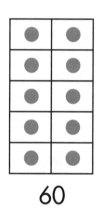 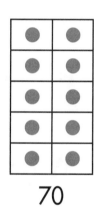 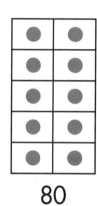 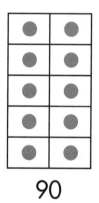

60   70   80   90

Trace and write 90.

90 _ _ _ _

Lesson 4.7 Counting and Writing 90

Count 90 apples. Circle each group of 10 apples. Draw a worm in apple 86.

Lesson 4.8 Counting and Writing 100

100 is ten groups of 10. Count 100 dots.

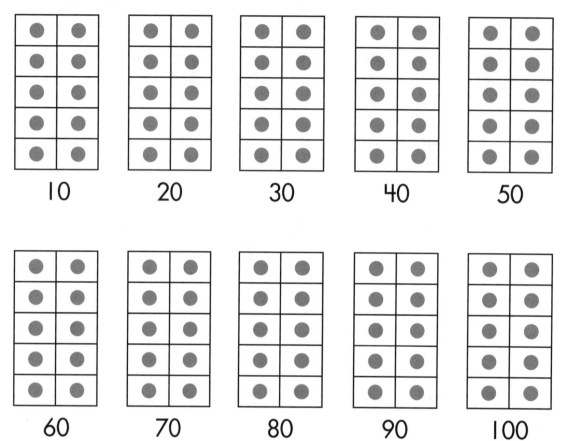

10   20   30   40   50

60   70   80   90   100

Trace and write 100.

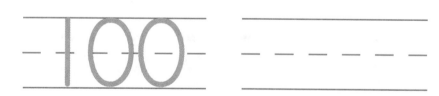

Lesson 4.8 Counting and Writing 100

Count 100 apples. Circle each group of 10 apples. Draw a worm in apple 99.

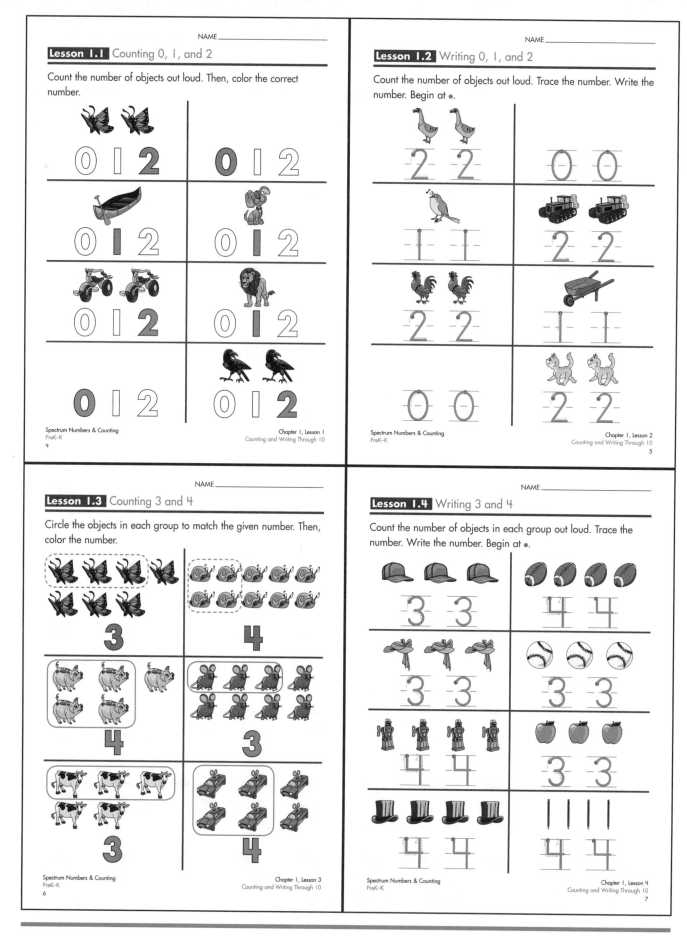

Spectrum Numbers & Counting
PreK–K

Answer Key

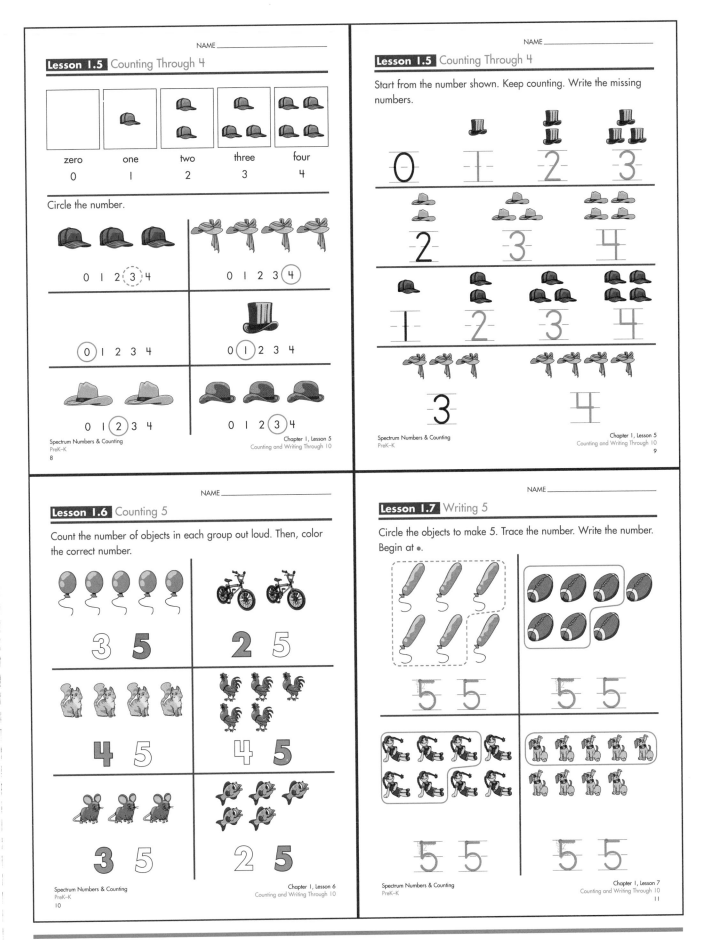

Lesson 1.5 Counting Through 4

zero	one	two	three	four
0	1	2	3	4

Circle the number.

0 1 2 (3) 4   0 1 2 3 (4)

(0) 1 2 3 4   0 (1) 2 3 4

0 1 (2) 3 4   0 1 2 (3) 4

Spectrum Numbers & Counting
PreK–K
8

Chapter 1, Lesson 5
Counting and Writing Through 10

Lesson 1.5 Counting Through 4

Start from the number shown. Keep counting. Write the missing numbers.

0   1   2   3

2   3   4

1   2   3   4

3   4

Spectrum Numbers & Counting
PreK–K

Chapter 1, Lesson 5
Counting and Writing Through 10
9

Lesson 1.6 Counting 5

Count the number of objects in each group out loud. Then, color the correct number.

3 **5**   **2** 5

4 5   4 **5**

3 5   2 **5**

Spectrum Numbers & Counting
PreK–K
10

Chapter 1, Lesson 6
Counting and Writing Through 10

Lesson 1.7 Writing 5

Circle the objects to make 5. Trace the number. Write the number. Begin at •.

5 5   5 5

5 5   5 5

Spectrum Numbers & Counting
PreK–K

Chapter 1, Lesson 7
Counting and Writing Through 10
11

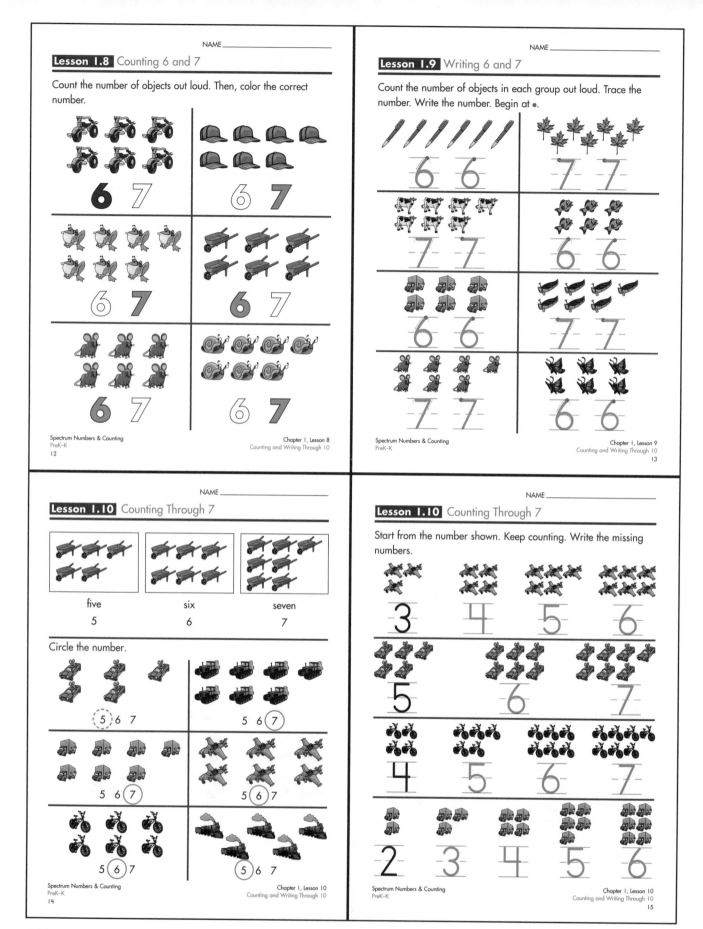

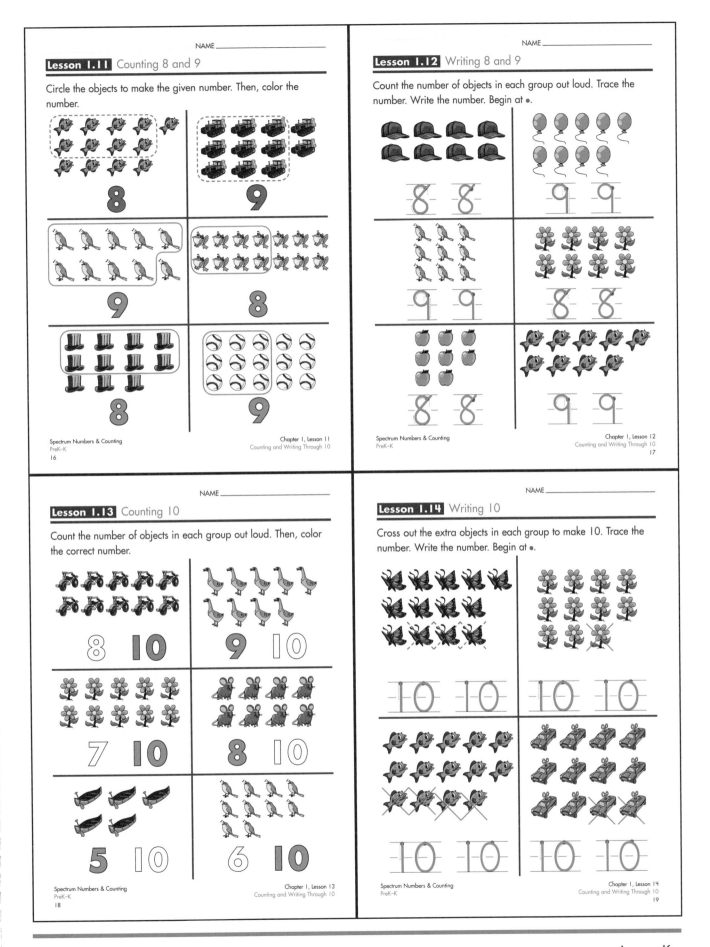

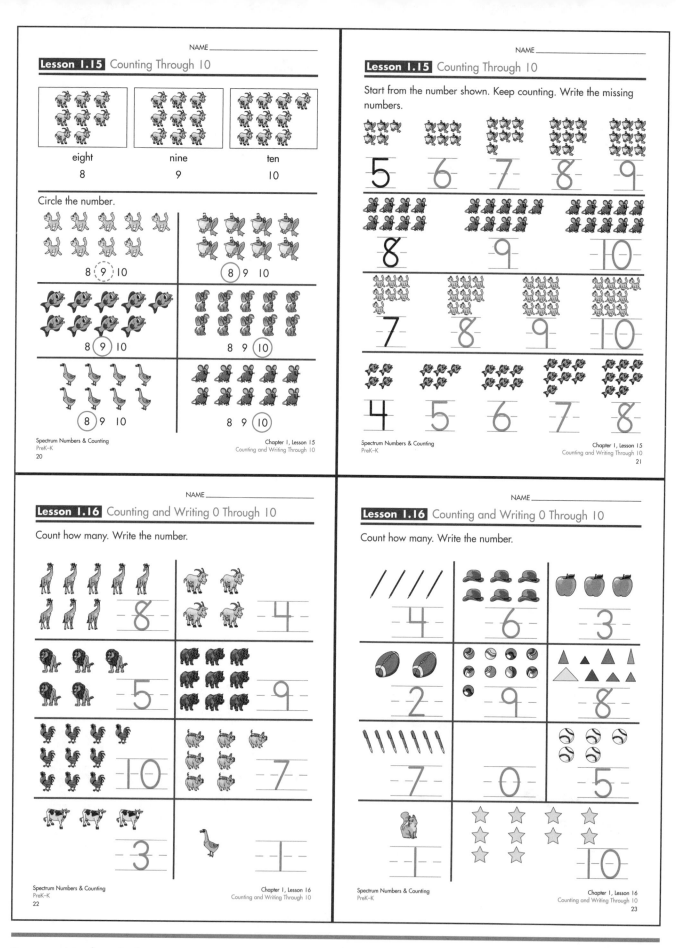

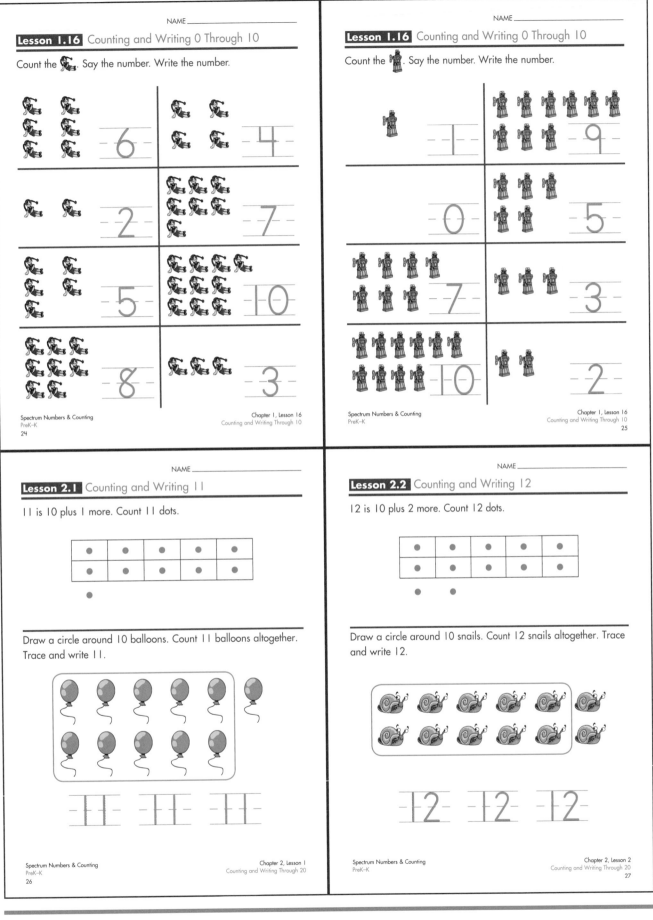

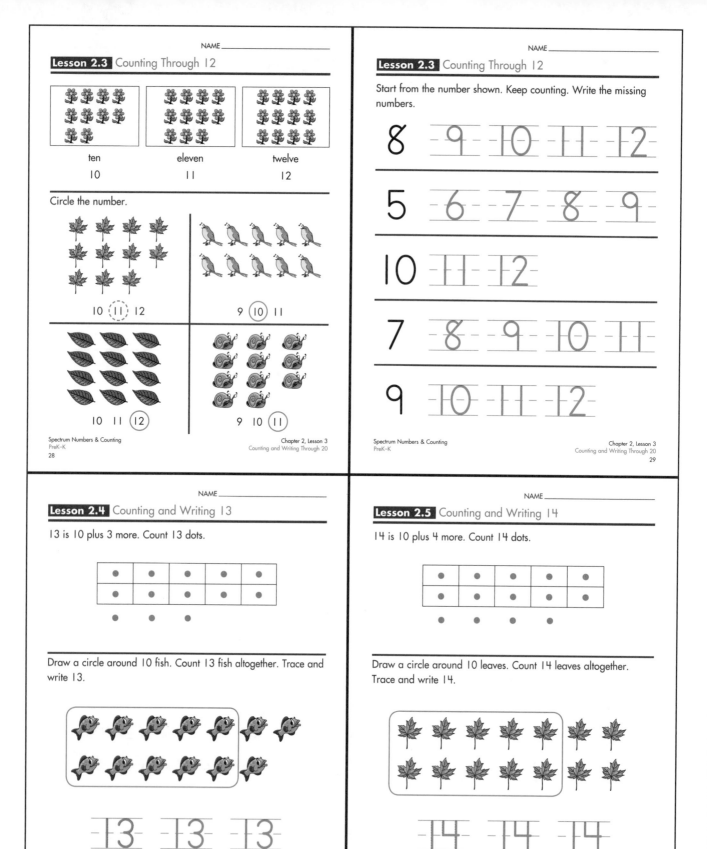

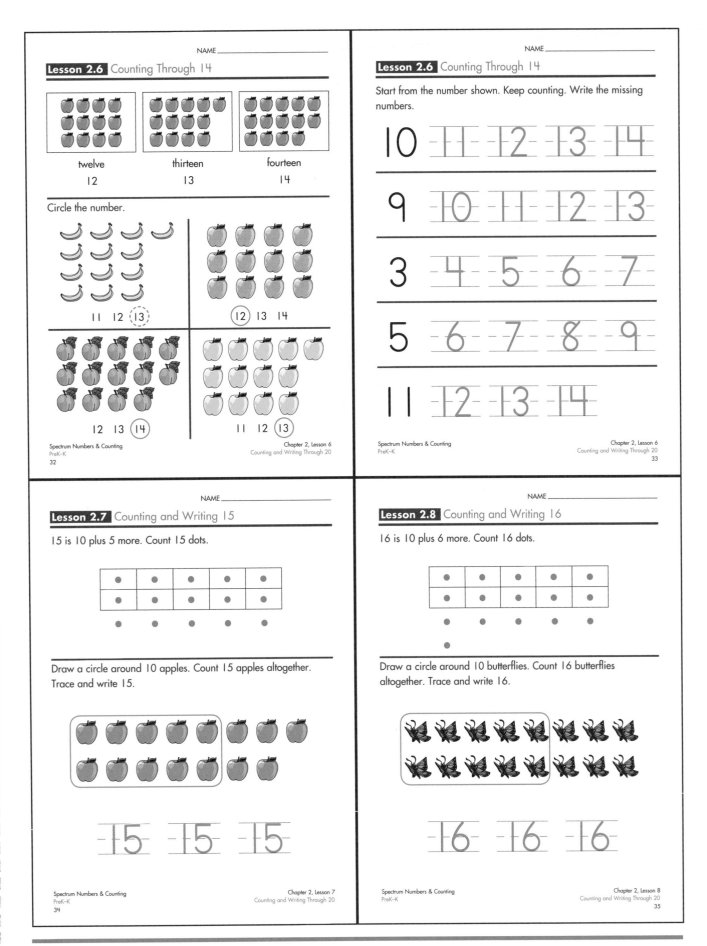

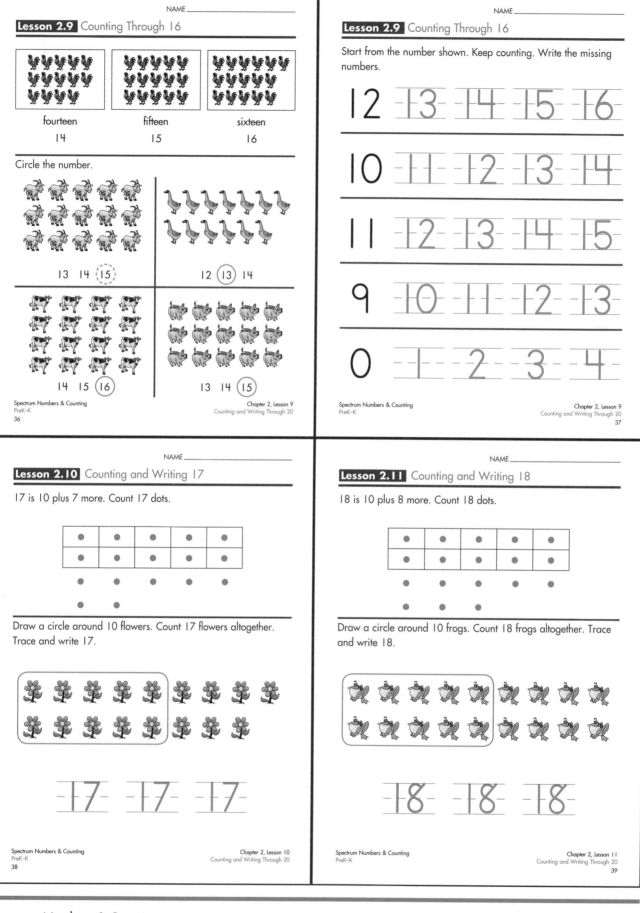

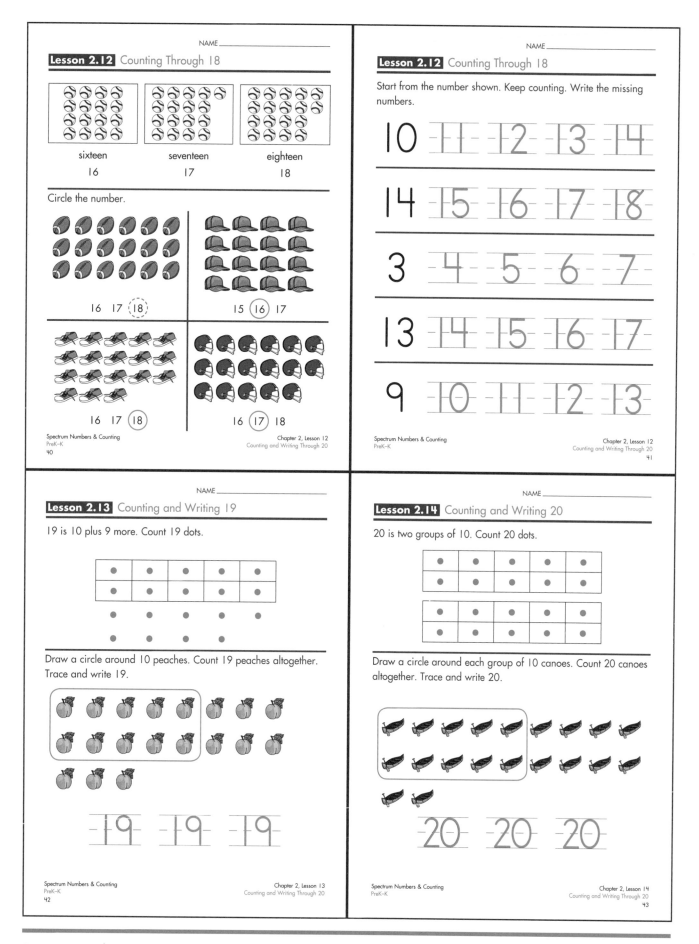

Lesson 2.12 Counting Through 18

sixteen seventeen eighteen
16 17 18

Circle the number.

16 17 (18)

15 (16) 17

16 17 (18)

16 (17) 18

Spectrum Numbers & Counting
PreK–K
40

Chapter 2, Lesson 12
Counting and Writing Through 20

Lesson 2.12 Counting Through 18

Start from the number shown. Keep counting. Write the missing numbers.

10 11 12 13 14

14 15 16 17 18

3 4 5 6 7

13 14 15 16 17

9 10 11 12 13

Spectrum Numbers & Counting
PreK–K

Chapter 2, Lesson 12
Counting and Writing Through 20
41

Lesson 2.13 Counting and Writing 19

19 is 10 plus 9 more. Count 19 dots.

Draw a circle around 10 peaches. Count 19 peaches altogether. Trace and write 19.

19 19 19

Spectrum Numbers & Counting
PreK–K
42

Chapter 2, Lesson 13
Counting and Writing Through 20

Lesson 2.14 Counting and Writing 20

20 is two groups of 10. Count 20 dots.

Draw a circle around each group of 10 canoes. Count 20 canoes altogether. Trace and write 20.

20 20 20

Spectrum Numbers & Counting
PreK–K

Chapter 2, Lesson 14
Counting and Writing Through 20
43

Spectrum Numbers & Counting
PreK–K

Answer Key

87

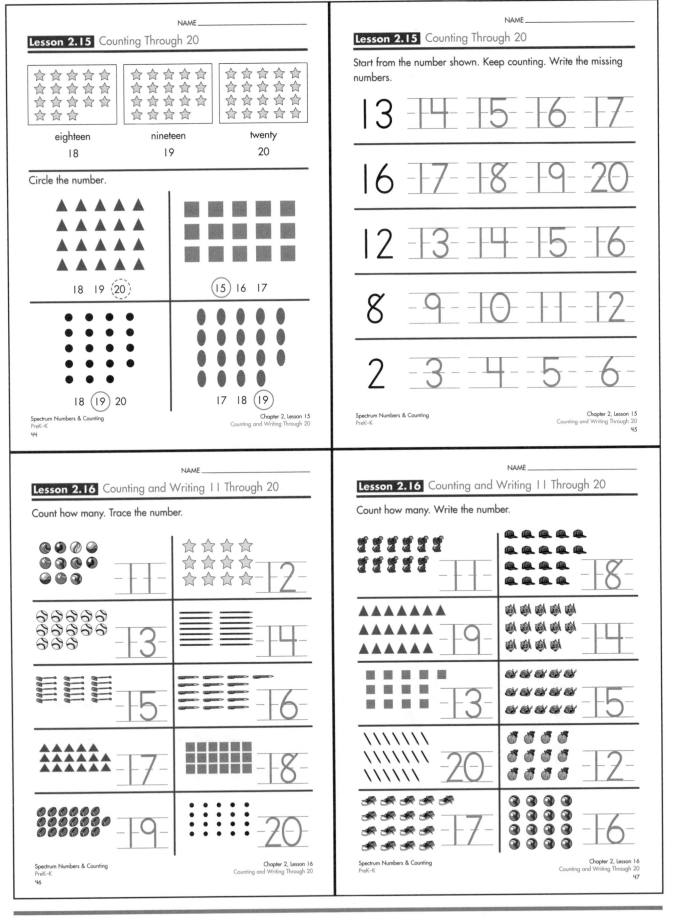

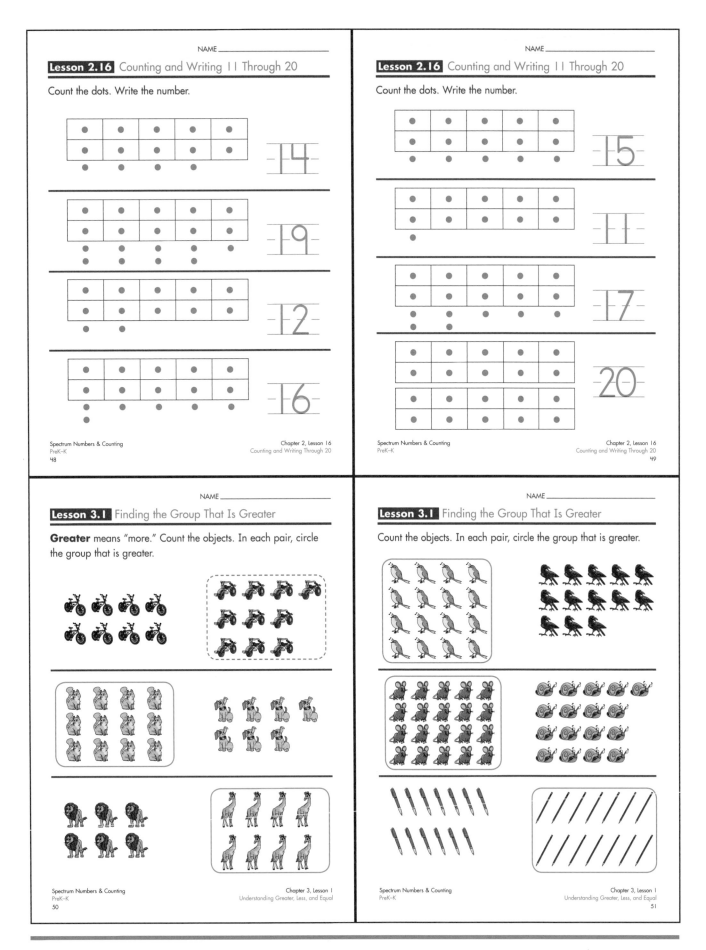

Spectrum Numbers & Counting
PreK–K

Answer Key

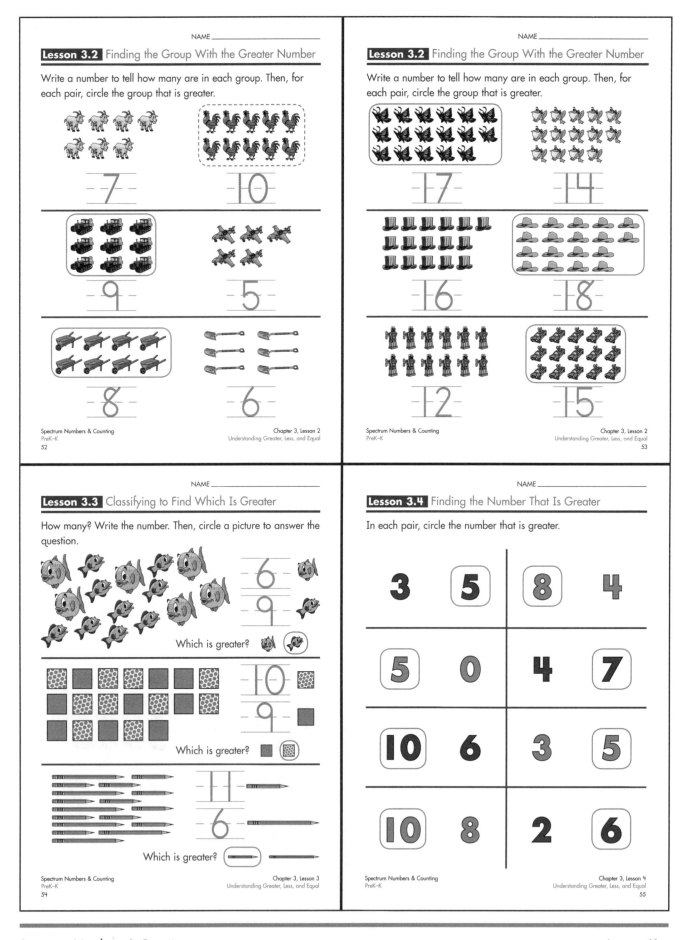

Lesson 3.5 Finding the Group That Is Less

Less means "fewer." Count the objects. In each pair, circle the group that is less.

Lesson 3.5 Finding the Group That Is Less

Count the objects. In each pair, circle the group that is less.

 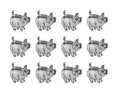

Lesson 3.6 Finding the Group With the Lesser Number

Write a number to tell how many are in each group. Then, for each pair, circle the group that is less.

 6 11

 10 13

 5 8

Lesson 3.6 Finding the Group With the Lesser Number

Write a number to tell how many are in each group. Then, for each pair, circle the group that is less.

20 16

4 7

10 15

Spectrum Numbers & Counting
PreK–K

Answer Key

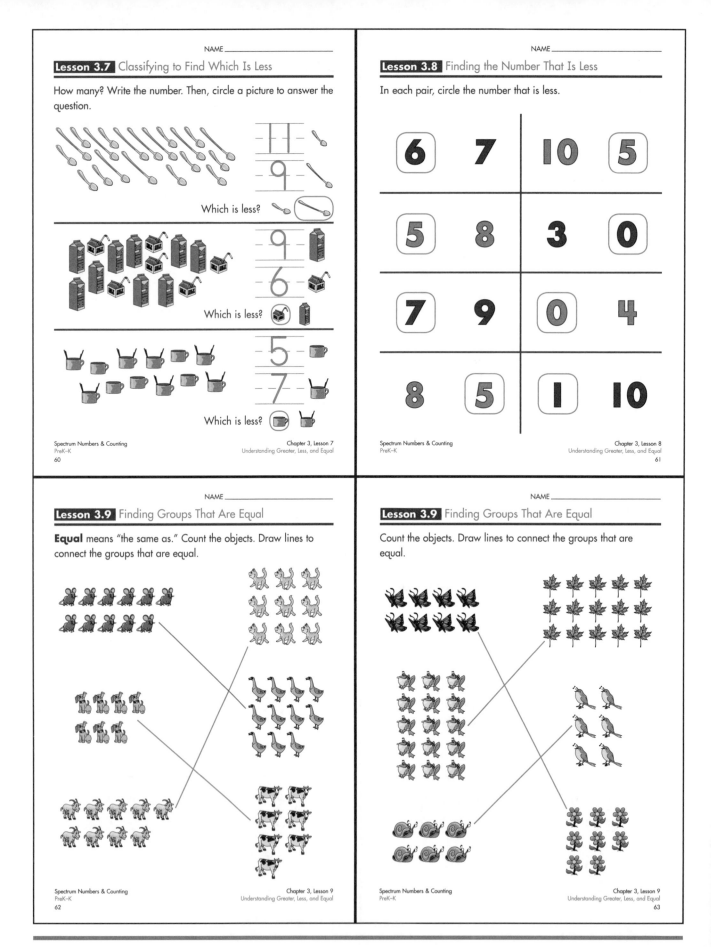

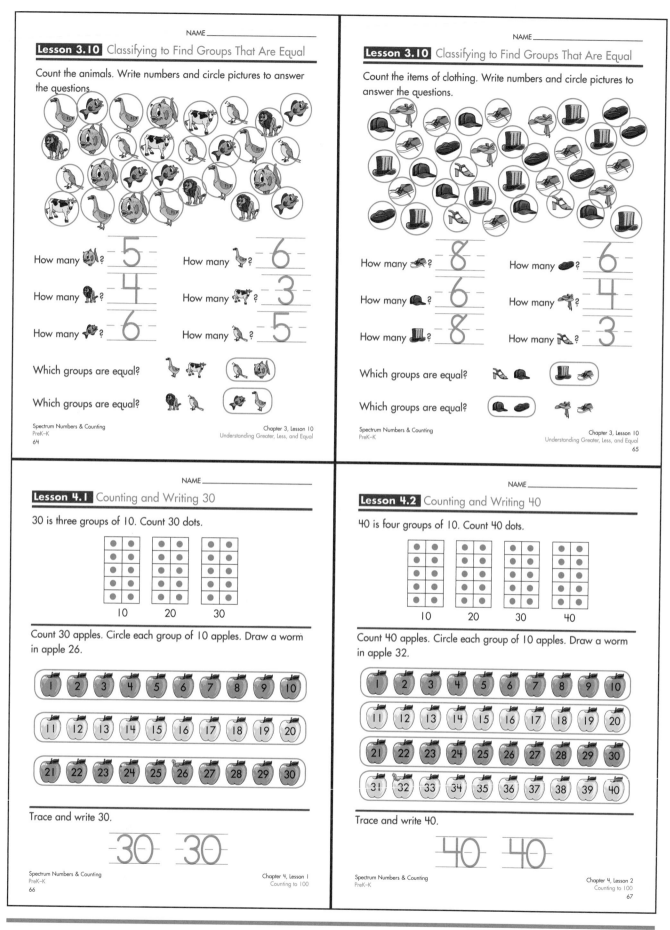

Lesson 3.10 Classifying to Find Groups That Are Equal

Count the animals. Write numbers and circle pictures to answer the questions.

How many 🐶? **5**   How many 🦆? **6**

How many 🦁? **4**   How many 🐄? **3**

How many 🐟? **6**   How many 🐦? **5**

Which groups are equal? 🦆 🐄   (🐦 🐶)

Which groups are equal? 🦁 🐦   (🐟 🦆)

Lesson 3.10 Classifying to Find Groups That Are Equal

Count the items of clothing. Write numbers and circle pictures to answer the questions.

How many 👟? **8**   How many 👞? **6**

How many 🧢? **6**   How many 🔫? **4**

How many 🎩? **8**   How many 👠? **3**

Which groups are equal? 👠 🧢   (🎩 👟)

Which groups are equal? (🧢 👞)   🎀 👟

Lesson 4.1 Counting and Writing 30

30 is three groups of 10. Count 30 dots.

10   20   30

Count 30 apples. Circle each group of 10 apples. Draw a worm in apple 26.

1 2 3 4 5 6 7 8 9 10

11 12 13 14 15 16 17 18 19 20

21 22 23 24 25 26 27 28 29 30

Trace and write 30.

30 30

Lesson 4.2 Counting and Writing 40

40 is four groups of 10. Count 40 dots.

10   20   30   40

Count 40 apples. Circle each group of 10 apples. Draw a worm in apple 32.

1 2 3 4 5 6 7 8 9 10

11 12 13 14 15 16 17 18 19 20

21 22 23 24 25 26 27 28 29 30

31 32 33 34 35 36 37 38 39 40

Trace and write 40.

40 40

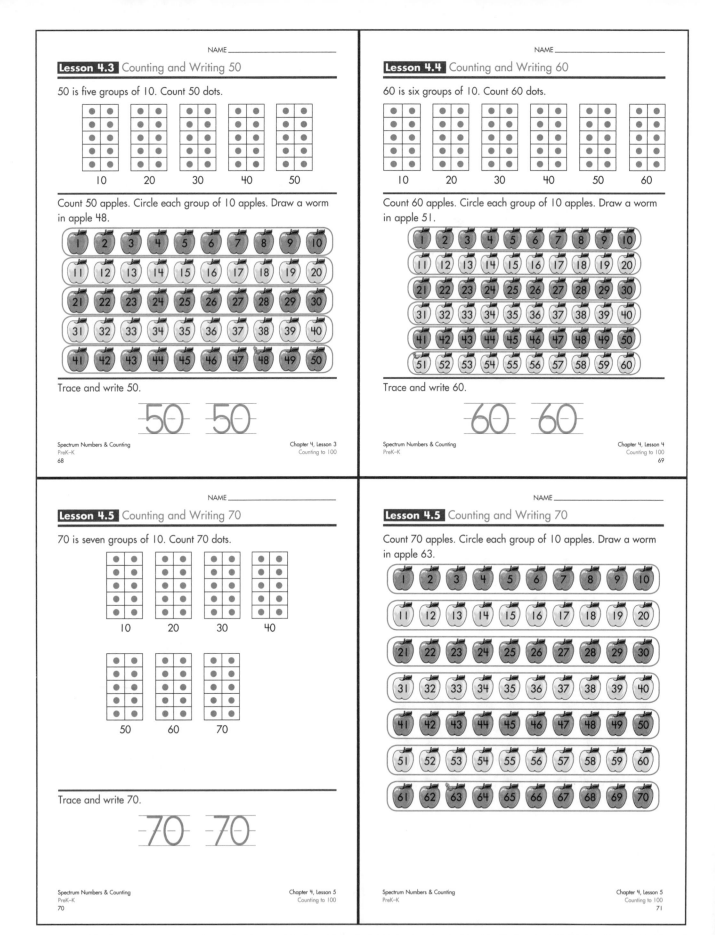

Lesson 4.3 Counting and Writing 50

50 is five groups of 10. Count 50 dots.

10   20   30   40   50

Count 50 apples. Circle each group of 10 apples. Draw a worm in apple 48.

Trace and write 50.

50 50

Lesson 4.4 Counting and Writing 60

60 is six groups of 10. Count 60 dots.

10   20   30   40   50   60

Count 60 apples. Circle each group of 10 apples. Draw a worm in apple 51.

Trace and write 60.

60 60

Lesson 4.5 Counting and Writing 70

70 is seven groups of 10. Count 70 dots.

10   20   30   40

50   60   70

Trace and write 70.

70 70

Lesson 4.5 Counting and Writing 70

Count 70 apples. Circle each group of 10 apples. Draw a worm in apple 63.

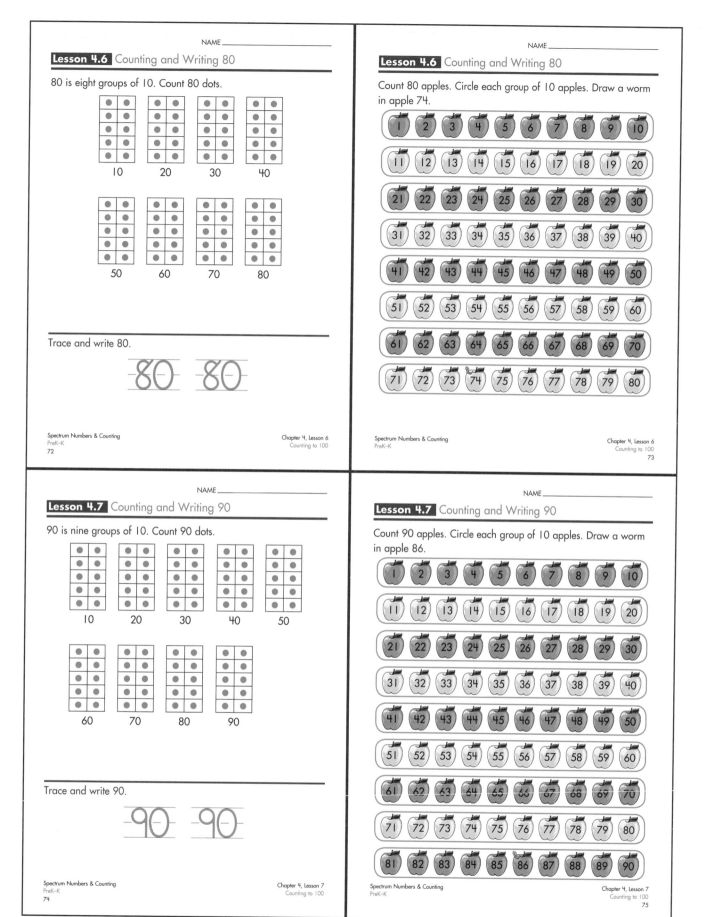

Lesson 4.8 Counting and Writing 100

100 is ten groups of 10. Count 100 dots.

10	20	30	40	50

60	70	80	90	100

Trace and write 100.

Lesson 4.8 Counting and Writing 100

Count 100 apples. Circle each group of 10 apples. Draw a worm in apple 99.

1	2	3	4	5	6	7	8	9	10
11	12	13	14	15	16	17	18	19	20
21	22	23	24	25	26	27	28	29	30
31	32	33	34	35	36	37	38	39	40
41	42	43	44	45	46	47	48	49	50
51	52	53	54	55	56	57	58	59	60
61	62	63	64	65	66	67	68	69	70
71	72	73	74	75	76	77	78	79	80
81	82	83	84	85	86	87	88	89	90
91	92	93	94	95	96	97	98	99	100
